FLIGHT OF FANTASY

By

Patricia L Graham

ReadMeDo

First Edition Published 2013 by: Lulu.com, 3101 Hillsborough Street, Raleigh, NC 27607, United States

In association with VerdanaBee: The Chandlery, Unit Office 501, 50 Westminster Bridge Road,

London SE1 7QY,

England

© Patricia L Graham 1983, 2011, 2012 and 2013

All Rights Reserved

ISBN: 978-1-291-38044-6

Printed and distributed by: Lulu.com

Pictures by: VerdanaBee

Logo by: Vistaprint

FLIGHT OF FANTASY COLLECTION

CONTENTS

Introduction	6
Stars Hug (Dedication)	8
Something in a Void	10
The Monkey and the Butterfly	11
The Audition	14
The Plight of a Dodo	25
The Wedding	33
They're Here, They're Watching	34
The Announcement	41
Last Days	42
Mother Earth	67
After the Aftermath	67
A Complicated Love	71
The End of the Hunt	75
The Tickled Bird	80
Out in the Cold	91
The Gallery of Life	92
The Spliced Continuum	100
Enigma	123

INTRODUCTION

About the Author

I have been writing since my teens and remember winning the school poetry prize for my year at secondary school. I couldn't read it out myself on account of a bad attack of flu. Later, life's events wrestled with me to the point that I struggled with my own ability to be creative and having other survival priorities.

Quite unexpectedly, this collection represents, by virtue of new technology, my first real attempt to reach out to a wider readership other than relatives, friends and acquaintances. I would however like to thank the Cambridge publisher with limited resources, who wrote that they would have liked to publish the very first full-length manuscript that I produced decades ago. Years later, I realise I would have needed to do more work on that draft which was not sci/fantasy related, but it is the thought that remains.

Sci/fantasy, like some other genres, allows exploration and reflection on a range of issues about human existence. I like to tackle these aspects every now and then and hope the reader enjoys this selection of short stories, flash fiction, poetry and drama written over the years. The core of my inspiration flows from my own spiritual beliefs. However, I was also inspired to put this collection together after engaging with fellow writers, most notably on ABCtales.com. This helped me to better hone my talents, something this modern age has facilitated by making tools which are geographically accessible on the internet.

"Last Days", "Mother Earth" and "After the Aftermath" were all written in the early 1980's. "Plight of a Dodo" was triggered by a Foyles 2012 Murakami competition which I did not enter but later took the opportunity to extend the word count. The "Gallery of Life" was written after I participated in a project run by the UK National Archives also in 2012 called *Caribbean through a Lens* which rather speaks for itself. Needless to say, I was much inspired.

I hope you find something that tickles your fancy in my collection.

Patricia L Graham

STARS HUG

Your seasonal innocence, shone so bright
In the hearts of those who shared your life
Stars hug the night
Sun rules the day
Your warmth, our memory will never change

Dedication: 2012 to 2013 for Jamaica's 50th Jubilee Anniversary of Independence

*The planet's rotation separates day from night
Divides the darkness from the light
Devotion set in Motion*

**Abba's Blessings Always
One Love …**

SOMETHING IN A VOID

For we perceive beyond the rainbow,
Beyond the shadow of gravity holding ISS.
Caught not in a void
But like bees wading in their own honey,
Pollinating space with thoughts …

Our tent did blow from on high
Exposing this nakedness.
They, uncomprehending,
A soul did incarcerate;
Feeding barest morsels shared with rats;
Though famished eyed her fleeting skirt.
So did she infiltrate his racked dreams?
Spittle healing cuts; kisses soothing bruises,
Milk nourishing hunger …
Tears washing away grimy sorrow.

Such comfort in the bounds of direst misery …

THE BUTTERFLY AND THE MONKEY

Shaggy and Noel joined Laura in the Bar. Shaggy was still jet lagged and Laura hadn't yet recovered from the party in the early hours. She had probably drunk way too much gin than she cared to remember and was suffering a thumping headache.

She frantically searched her handbag for a quick fix remedy. Noel suggested perhaps a coffee would be better than a pill. Shaggy had ordered a cup of Earl Grey bergamot tea which had just arrived.

"That smells nice," Laura blearily remarked. "Maybe I'll have one of those, so long as it doesn't come with milk, cream or sugar."

Shaggy passed her his cup and ordered another. She thanked him and jadedly slipped a teaspoon into the chiming china, slowly stirring unnecessary swirling eddies.

The bartender turned on the rotor blade fan to the clink of glasses. No one noticed when the butterfly floated in, landing gracefully on Laura's teaspoon before her kente coloured form slid into the fluid, first bathing the tips of her waterproof wings until she disappeared completely.

She finally emerged through the tiniest of whirlpools and with her compound eyes scanned wet fingertips as monkey scooped up some water to drink. He blinked twice, astonished by this colourful apparition, stunned by her scent. Before he could say Bob's your uncle, she flitted through his butterfingers, wafting away in the direction of the forest.

Monkey shot up from crouching, abruptly aware of his eligibility and drawn to follow the scent of her trail. This was crazy and he knew it. Everyone would say it was impossible to fall in love in an instant but to fall in love with a butterfly was just plain balmy. He scaled his lofty thoughts as the sun's steely rays burned her trail. Monkey suddenly realised he had lost the scent and sight of his elusive butterfly. A pang of grief struck him. He felt lost and alone, betrayed even.

It then came to him that the elephants, who had long memories and practised the art of law-faring in the jungle, to the south, might have a clue as to what he should do. The elephants lived in a land where a variety of monkeys were also fabled to live. Why, he'd even become a butterfly too if it came to it, if she'd have him, despite only momentarily having been slightly aware of his entire existence much less his intent mind you.

There was a tapping, Noel was tapping Laura's cup.

"Someone needs to get home to bed I think."

"Hmm." Shaggy raised an eyebrow.

"Think you're right," yawned Laura. "I have a story to write about how a monkey met his future wife in the land of elephants of all places."

The two men looked at her with bemusement.

"Pardon?" both asked.

"Never mind … Just a short story, all forty winks of it. Great tea by the way."

THE AUDITION

ACT ONE

Actors: *(in order of appearance)*

    Director
    Usher
    Alice

Scene One

(At a well lit theatre ...)

Director: Who's up next?

Usher: A young lady called Alice Director.

Director: Alice Nobody?

Usher: No Alice Peabody.

Director: She the last?

Usher: Actually she's the first, and the last.

Director: What happened to all the rest?

Usher: They were abducted Director.

Director: Abducted? By whom?

Usher: It seems aliens abducted them.

(Director, ponders, raises hand to chin, long list of names in hand, and glances at the paperwork.)

Director: All these people ... Does our government know about this?

Usher: We tried to contact them but they were all in a bunker in Colorado.

Director: Well, keep trying. Can't have this sort of thing happening when I've got a play to put on. Well, get Alice Nobody.

Usher: Peabody Mr Director, she insists.

Director: Get Alice Peabody in here then.

(Usher calls Alice. She enters and stands in front of the mike.)

Director: So Alice, what are you going to read for us?

Alice: From my script Director, it's called "Loggerheads".

Director: Good title. I like it, full of tension.

Alice: Thank you Mr Director.

Director: Alice, is there any reason why you're wearing that tin contraption on your head?

Alice: Oh that's just so I can contact my agent.

Director: Alice, we have phones for that these days. Hello …

Alice: Yes I know but the aliens don't like them.

Director: The aliens?

Alice: Why yes Mr Director, they abducted my agent while she was on a train on her way home but gave me this helmet so I could keep in touch with her.

Director: Very fetching Alice. Makes you look like an android.

Alice: Robot Mr Director, they prefer that word.

Director: Robot then, in the word according to the aliens.

Alice: I'm sure they'd appreciate that Mr Director.

Director: You really believe in aliens Alice?

Alice: Like a large percentage of Americans Mr Director, I sure do.

Director: But this is the UK Alice, surely Brits don't believe that.

Alice: The trend is Brits believe everything Americans do too and luvin' it.

Director: Well that's just dandy Alice. Read Alice, read. Unless there's something else …

Alice: Well, I've waited so long, I'm afraid I'm now feeling partial to a cup of tea. That's if it's no trouble.

Director: A cup of tea?

Alice: Yes Director. No milk. *(Nods)*

Director: Why you got something against milk Alice?

Alice: Not at all Mr Director, just lactose intolerant.

Director: I see. Somebody get this woman a cup of black tea please.

Alice: Pardon me Director, but your voice sounded impatient when you said woman.

Director: It did?

Alice: Yes it did Director. I have to inform you that if you insist on stressing about my womanhood in that manner, I'll have to call my lawyer who is also a woman and

	doesn't like that sort of thing any more than I do and she's not even lactose intolerant.
Director:	I meant no offence Alice.
Alice:	None taken Director. You see my biology teacher also told us that race is not about colour, race is about blood, only the knowledgeable people don't know about it because they're too busy being knowledgeable about everything else to know if you understand what I mean.
Director:	To be perfectly honest Alice, no I don't understand.
Alice:	Well, we didn't understand him either on account of the fact that he didn't speak good English and being a science teacher and all, but we understood this part: phenotype is what you look like and genotype is actually what you are, everything else is ignorance.
Director:	Alice we don't have all day for this.
Usher:	Actually we do Mr Director as the others were abducted.

Director: *(Shaking his head)* Alice, I know who I am.

Alice: I'm sure you do Mr Director, but the question is after all, do you know who your parents were?

Director: Of course I know who my parents were. They raised me!

Alice: That's just it Mr Director. I'm getting a message they were not who you thought they were. They were in fact a pair of mischievous aliens by the name of Freddie and Fannie, destined to cause mayhem that would lead to global collapse.

Director: Alice, Alice ... You have parents too don't you?

Alice: I have One Father and He knows everything.

Director: *(Exasperated)* I bet he does at that.
(Softly) Alice are you about to start reading any time soon?

Alice: Actually, presently Mr Director. In a moment so to speak.

Director: What's wrong with right now Alice?

Alice: Well that depends on one's perspective Mr Director. Now was moments ago already so technically that's in the past presently which leaves me with the problem of when you would like me to start – again, the future not being ours to see relatively speaking or not being the present case. Just a theory …

Director: For Pete's sake Alice, are you taking the mick? Are you making this up as you go along Alice? *(The usher's name is also Pete)*

Alice: Since you mention it Mr Director, being a writer that's exactly right. By editing I can make it all up as I go along.

Director: I get the point Alice. Perhaps you could start reading for us sometime this century? When you feel comfortable. That help you out any?

Alice: Perfectly Mr Director. Thank you for your patience.

(She clears her throat and begins …)

Alice: Alice stepped through the looking glass.

Director: No wait! Alice stepped through the looking glass? You mean your key character is also called Alice, Alice?

Alice: Why yes, absolutely Mr Director. She is a reflection after all and this is a looking glass story you know.

Director: Okay, okay.

Alice: Alice stepped through the looking glass and onto the chessboard and disintegrated the whole board immediately.

Director: Just a minute Alice – you can't do that!

Alice: I can do anything I want Mr Director, I'm the author of this story. Remember?

Director: Yes Alice but this is England and that's just not cricket.

Alice: Never played cricket so I'm none too sure what you're getting at.

Director: But that's not the point Alice … it is the point. The point is you just can't go into looking glass world and just destroy the game before it has even played out. There's a whole history of this game going back to India or Egypt even if we include senet.

Alice: Do I look Egyptian to you Mr Director?

Director: I didn't say you look Egyptian Alice, as I previously recall saying you look like an android/ err robot.

Alice: Yes, in all fairness you did. Well that's the point Mr Director. It's all an illusion. There is no chessboard.

Director: No chessboard?

Alice: No. Never was. Everyone knows the world is just a big onion. All you have to do is peel one to see it just keeps going round in circles. The aliens say what goes around comes around.

Director: And who exactly revealed this great secret?

Alice: Oh I believe that was Tammy. Why Tammy told everyone Mr Director – didn't you hear that recorded message?

Director: I must have been playing around in a bunker somewhere. There any more of your story to read Alice?

Alice: That's the beginning and end of it Mr Director. Learnt to do that recently. So I've edited the chessboard completely as we've been speaking. Right ... *(Shuffles)* the story now reads ... in a moment: "The world is an onion. Full stop."

Director: Thank you Alice. Everybody out to lunch! Pronto!

THE END

THE PLIGHT OF A DODO

"A young man carries his bag.
He travels alone, his destination unclear."

Kado remembered reading these words when he was younger, yet here he was in the moment, living the words he had retained for some obscure reason.

He had snapped out of his reverie as the alarm sounded. His father was playing that haunting tune *(ELP's: The Sage)*. Those words too pulsated around his cranium, triggering his otherwise dulled synapses.

His day had arrived. It was time to leave. He pressed the penultimate airlock button, stepping closer into the unknown. The bag was concealed inside his hazmat suit. He did not know how long the meagre provisions it held would last but was optimistic as invincible young men could muster in his time. He closed the last airlock door and headed clumsily straight for the ridge ahead of him. It was all his now vacant mind could focus on. No one would come after him. He did not look back for there was no turning back. This much about himself he had managed to salvage, despite the boredom of the past months which had been practically terminal: it was decisively over for him. Everyone he had cared about had perished. There was nothing more precious for him to lose, save his own life.

Multi-directional meteor-like showers had blasted out of the skies, hammering the planet, lacing the atmosphere with an aerosol spawned from vapour trails while laying thin purple blankets of powdery dust on the ground. The shockwave energy from these destructive forces had caused deaths, thousands of casualties and widespread infrastructure damage on a global scale. But the plague that ensued wiped out billions of people worldwide within two weeks. This was no Ebola, H1N1, SARS, Spanish Flu or Smallpox. No one was untouched. The Annihilation unfolded on the streets, on TV and on the Web till there was no one left with strength enough to report on it in earnest. Within a month it was global.

None of the satellites had picked up this incoming onslaught. Then the Havens had miraculously appeared. It was uncanny how people easily drifted into accepting their new circumstances. He had surfed enough conspiracy theory sites not to believe everything he had been told, but the devastation visited upon populations completely overrode any sense of right, wrong or injustice. There was only survival left and you took it out of desperation; like a zombie programmed to live. That's how it felt to begin with. It had taken Kado twenty months to succumb to the feeling he could only describe as being a pervading plague itself of repetitive sheer boredom. Perversely, it was part of the fabric of life in the engineered protective biosphere, which had also deflated any desire within Kado to even procreate. However, this was not an issue for the authorities who weekly demanded he produce a cone of sperm at his leisure by preference, with a tablet if he had any difficulties complying, otherwise an injection was the final alternative. The latter two options did not appeal to him and as women were now deemed more essential for other tasks, he unwillingly complied. Memories of Hikaru invaded his mind at such times; she still lived in his blood, leaving him spent.

Survival this way for Kado was meaningless and unbearable. Was it living, just to be cooped up breathing regurgitated air? Watching rerun movies of life the way it had been. It made him feel like a Dodo. This regimented existence in such a sterile environment, some said was understandably so to conserve energy and to ration supplies. The industry of breathing had of necessity devoured the former industry of consumerism. For Kado the essential effort to stay alive had totally exhausted overnight.

In his bag he carried the sum total of his worldly possessions which he had hurriedly thrown together without much of a selection process: pictures of his parents and girlfriend, the family cat; a couple bottles of water, some nutrition pills and a few pastes – six weeks' supply should he last that long; antiseptic wipes.

He, together with a friend, had found themselves caught in England on a lifetime break when the events broke out. The landscape was now completely transformed. Greenbelt land had morphed into something akin to a scene from Laredo, without enough body bags to bury a whole country. There was something in the way they started to drill people that had alerted him that all was not right with the reports. For awhile he was able to push such thoughts to the back of his mind.

Now however, he was walking away from life, to precarious and very likely imminent death by leaving the security of his nightshift processing station. He had taken this decision by volunteering to finish off a colleague's work. Jiro, his friend, still harboured the hope of engaging one of the native girls in food processing. That was a joke because everything eaten now came in a tube or tablet mostly, the way the astronauts used to consume vital nutrients, only humans still lived on Terra Firma – no problems with extra payload. Perhaps the next generation would have no need for stomachs. Jiro could also find himself a candidate for chemical castration or worse, Kado tried to warn him. Maybe keeping his blood hot was what kept Jiro alive. He at least didn't have problems with the routine otherwise. Jiro was decidedly 'grateful'.

Kado had given no indication to his colleagues he would not see them again, particularly Jiro. He was simply past caring, though an iota enough for Jiro to not prolong the agony of leaving. Was this suicide or just his way of accelerating the inevitable? He was undecided. This was foremost escape.

The sun still shone, though northern lights could be seen more southerly now. You could catch a glimpse outside the reinforced Haven glass. Outside the dome it danced magnificently across the whole vault of the distant sky as far as he could see, beautifully magnetic. Perhaps he was answering its hypnotic call.

He had by now put some distance between himself and the shelter. He estimated he had been walking for at least an hour. The desolate landscape appeared tranquil. Thus far he had not noticed any telling symptoms. A slight wind was now whipping around his visor. His suit was already uncomfortably hot. He would have to remove it. He took a deep breath. It could well be one of his last.

He rapidly breathed in and out; the only sound, his breathing interlaced with a whistling wind. There were no birds, no visible animals or even creeping things. After the safety of his incarceration, the wind reminded him of what it really felt like to be alive; perhaps how it felt to be born even but between the clefts of sterile looking mountains.

He closed his eyes. The symptoms were supposed to be rapid, he knew what to expect. He began to feel a tickling in his throat, wondering if this was the first sign. The sun suddenly blinked black.

He felt a trickle on his face. He shifted, instinctively moving his hand to wipe the fluid away. Unbeknown to him he had emerged from a coma, though still outdoors. He squinted as he could not believe his eyes. He patted around for his bag, for reassurance of his sanity. He pinched himself but the image did not budge. A strange hand reached out to him. Kado did not take it. He was too afraid to. The hand's owner had a body that looked like the swirling gases on Jupiter encased in a bright golden aura. With a Cyclops eye, the age old storm examined him. The owner retrieved its hand, before gaseous forming lips converged to utter words.

"Welcome traveller … You are the first to emerge from the Haven for ten months. I am Rai. We have been expecting you." The voice sounded like a zong reverberating from deep space but Kado had no problems understanding. He sweated.

"Expecting me? Who are you? What are you?" He asked nervously, trembling.

"What no thanks for saving your life then?"

"Was I looking to be saved?" He found himself gaining a little confidence. It was his life they were talking about after all, that life that had been ebbing away.

"The state you were in ... Anyway, there's no time for all that now. I am obliged to inform you that you have passed the third initiative test and must now proceed quickly to the next stage."

"Proceed to what? Did the plague kill me? Did the plague kill you? Am I still alive?"

"So you believed in the plague?"

"No I didn't."

"Why bring the subject up then?"

Kado was agitated by these concentric riddles. The being suggested he would not need his bag, or any of its contents. Kado shakily rose to his feet. He collected his thoughts before making a move in Rai's direction. It suddenly occurred to him that if there was no plague, why should he just follow this being simply because he was invited to? He stood his ground. Rai sensed this and turned to confront him.

"So, you prefer to be alone, when there are others like you waiting. Don't you want to meet them?"

"I'm happy to wait it out right here. You haven't told me a single thing worth knowing yet."

"Feisty I must say. Maybe you would prefer to fight, that your style? How about some jujitsu?"

"What makes you think I learnt jujitsu and fight for what? Anything worth fighting for is gone." With that remark he plopped back down to the ground, coughing because of the dust his resolve had thrown up.

Without glancing back, Rai instructed him to wait. Another would come for him shortly. He had apparently passed the Fourth Level without even following.

Kado contemplated perhaps he had died. He couldn't figure out what kind of game was being played on him. Or maybe he hadn't escaped from the Haven after all. Somehow he had been retrieved and was pumped full of psychotropic drugs. Whatever this was, he did not know the rules. He was definitely intrigued to learn more. His first step had been to choose to live without fear. However, his sense of boredom had completely evaporated. He felt extremely alive again and his pulse was racing.

The sun was setting. He had swallowed food, drank water sparingly and relieved himself. His body was fully functioning. He waited restlessly. The sun set and darkness fell. He waited. The stars gradually spread across the night until the moon appeared, drifting over Orion's Belt where she started falling; down, down, down she fell until she hit the horizon and began striding towards Kado. He recognised her gait ... Hikaru ... Hikaru he muttered tentatively. He could always spot those dancing feet from a mile away. It had to be Hikaru. She was alive ...

THE WEDDING

It was everywhere and nowhere. She walked up the aisle alone. The carpet was deeply red and the sun shone through the glass, filtering down and across the high ceiling.

She glided past the old women sat facing the aisle. She smiled. They were the only three people in the congregation but dressed perfectly for the occasion. Two were already deceased and the third, unbeknown to herself, would join them months later. The bride had washed all their feet, prepared them for the inevitable.

No one could see the groom, though his presence was unmistakable. They were married and went outside. The stupendous building was supported by huge pillars. Samson would have been proud when she pushed the pillars and they gave way, destabilising the whole edifice which crashed and crumbled.

It was finished. She smiled across the valley below.

THEY'RE HERE, THEY'RE WATCHING

ACT ONE

SCENE ONE

(Two MI5 operatives are on surveillance duty in a white van outside a suspect's house who is an old lady.)

Actors:　　No1
　　　　　　No2
　　　　　　Alien Bear

No1　So are you married?

No2　No, never married and no children.

No1　Me neither. You think that's why they selected us for this assignment?

No2　I don't know. My father died years ago but my mother is in a nursing home. I do see her when I can find the time though.

No1 I have a sister, but we haven't seen each other since we had an argument over my father's Will, my mother having died years prior. I guess if anything happened here, it's not like anyone would miss us immediately like. Know what I'm saying?

No2 You think we're expendable? Why should anything happen on this job? Remind me why we're here again.

No1 Well the hidden camera keeps conking out or else the neighbours are in on what's going on.

No2 In on what? In on what exactly?

No1 That's what we're trying to find out.

No2 So how do we think the neighbours are involved anyway?

No1 Ahh, their pets keep showing up on the film. We figure they must be trained to do that.

No2 Pets?

No1 Yeh pets – you know, cats and dogs. Not at the same time mind you, the cats and the dogs that

	is but mainly it's the cats because cats are like that.
No2	You don't say … *(He nods)*
No1	I do say. I mean do bears poop in the woods or what?
No2	Right. But we don't have any bears in UK woods.
No1	That a fact?
No2	Yes it is.
No1	So, anyway cats just love having their picture taken apparently. Loads of film with their furry mugs and not much else.
No2	So why not just move the cameras out of the way of the cats and the dogs?
No1	Oh they tried that.
No2	*(Waiting)* So what happened?

No1   Well the other wildlife joined in.

No2   Other wildlife?

No1   Yeh the birds – magpies in particular. Now the magpies, they didn't want their pictures taken.

No2   They didn't?

No1   No they did not. So they started leaving their droppings over the lens. Real messy.

No2   How about that!

No1   Yeh, that's how we knew like with the cats and the dogs, especially the cats mind, they were all in it with the old woman over there.

No2   I see. And what do we think she's up to?

No1   Oh she's an alien.

No2   An alien? You mean like an illegal migrant right?

No1   Nah, nah! Not 'alf! She's one of them extra terrestrials, real ET type.

No2   You're kidding!

No1   No! And we suspect the wildlife around here, they're also ET's. That's why they decided to put a hands on crew on the job. We think she's got a runabout craft in the back of her garden. The real neighbours kept reporting strange lights at night.

No2   Oh they did?

No1   Yeh. Hold up, you hear that noise?

No2   Sounds like a chopper. Probably one of our guys making their rounds.

(The street suddenly goes black.)

SCENE TWO

(They emerge in space, gradually.)

No1   Hey, what's going on? There a blackout or something?

No2   I don't know. I'll take a look. *(Opens the door and closes it quickly.)*

No1   Well? What did you see?

No2   I must be dreaming. *(Rubs his forehead.)*

No1   Come on what did you see?!

No2   Is that the Earth rising in the rear view mirror?

No1   What?! *(He looks and certainly the Earth is out there.)* What is going on?! Where are we?!

No2   I'd say it looks like the moon man!

No1   So what now? You think they'll come rescue us or maybe we have our own bases up here already or something?

No2   I wouldn't hold my breath! Well, look at it this way, we're in a white van on the moon and none of this equipment cost trillions to get us here. What do you think?

No1   I think we best check our alien manuals to make sure we say the right thing when they come and get us. If they're still making out they're cats we can start with a meow. But no stroking, it may not be culturally correct if they're in control up here like the Egyptians had that Bes thing going on.

No2   Yeh, yeh and the dog Anubis.

(The door opens. It's an alien bear.)

No1   Anything in the manual about bears?

No2   We killed them all out in the UK so no … Sorry.

Ends

THE ANNOUNCEMENT

It was 2012, somewhere in Babylon. She stood up and walked to the rostrum.

"Ladies and gentlemen, I have an announcement to make." She spoke deeply into the mike.

"Before I leave this room today, there is something I really need to say. It has recently come to my attention that there are rumours about me and my association with Boneheads. I want to make it perfectly clear that I have never been a member of the Bonehead Cone Alliance. I also want to make it absolutely clear that I am not married to a Bonehead and that includes secretly. Never, not now or at any time past did I marry a Bonehead. There is certainly no secret marriage. That is not to say that I have anything against Boneheads. Some of my friends are Boneheads and Cones too, though I have never been to their homes for dinner." She cleared her throat before continuing.

"I think that about covers it. That's all I have to say on the matter. Thank you for allowing me the opportunity to set the record straight. Thank you for your time and kindness."

LAST DAYS

Introduction – narrated by a Primal

My only wish is to put you on your guard. We Primals once lived on a world lusciously vibrant with an abundant diversity of life, both flora and fauna. In an inkling of the time our planet took to evolve, all this was starkly transformed by death and destruction on a scale we could scarce imagine. You may be wondering how this could have happened in paradise. If you knew my people, you would understand, we had neither the capacity nor the inclination to bring about such devastation. For thousand of years, our ancestors lived in harmony with the provisions nature provided. That which destroyed our world, first came from without, working its way relentlessly within.

Our planet was probably somewhat smaller than your world, with one large continent, no ice caps; the climate tropical, supporting a population of around 4.5 million. There were no destructive storm systems, active volcanoes or earthquake zones. The life forms on our world were benign by your standards, all vegetarians, including insects. There were no large predators. We dreamed of living past one hundred years old, long enough to see our grandchildren grow up. The deep sleep, you call death, to us was a natural process of aging. We had few untreatable diseases, illnesses were seldom fatal. Most sudden deaths were either caused by unfortunate accidents or carelessness.

We worshipped the Mother Essence and the Universal Father in the greater expanse of the heavens, both visible and invisible. We thought we had a relatively good life, unaware we were in the stone-age. We lived in villages, initially were monogamous by design, men and women working together according to their strengths and abilities. Our regional societies depended on mutual co-operation. Whoever demonstrated the necessary attributes led by consensus regardless of gender.

Admittedly, we were far from perfect beings, having our differences. As time passed, these became more pronounced. Some believed it was because we had become discontented with our lot, straying from the old ways, that disaster inflicted itself upon us without mercy. Perhaps we ourselves had called the darkness into existence.

It began when female birth-rates dramatically increased, including a significant rise in twins. Our men demanded more power, insisting on polygamy to help redress the balance. In certain tribes, if the first birth was that of twin girls, it was condemned as evil. This was to culminate in the initiation of strange rituals, which necessitated the babies being put to death. Naturally, these practices impacted on our women in ways the ancestors would have been ashamed to see. It was not long before our diverging differences led to fierce outbreaks of tribal warfare.

Little did we know this was just the beginning of our woes.

Chapter 1

Legends have it, when the Archetype Andulakuns first arrived, they were strange looking beings, 8ft to 12ft giants; a cross between a reptile and a fish. There were approximately only three hundred of them. Perhaps none of us would have survived their onslaught, but for the fact that they seemed unable to withstand lengthy exposure to our atmosphere, their breathing being extremely laboured, forcing them to withdraw every thirty minutes.

The first tribes that encountered them instinctively ran. Months before there had been reports of strange omens in the sky, but we had no real understanding of how they came to our world. Some would have paid homage to these demons, but for their vile stench; putrid, like rotting fish mixed with catarrh. In a confined space it lingered, toxic and asphyxiating, as if we were being drained of the very air in our lungs. Our pregnant women were particularly susceptible, fainting in their presence.

Some tribes wanted to wage war against them with our futile bows and spears, but the Andulakuns aptly demonstrated their advanced weaponry. Their arsenal boasted brilliant fire that trail-blazed across the sky like meteor torches, descending on our villages: winged serpents, burning our reed and bamboo huts to ashes. They convincingly utilised the magic, might and power of their technology, in their swift subjugation of our world. Through this baptism, we experienced the real meaning of fear; of terror. It was not long before we learnt that their most effective offensives against our people were their diseases, which decimated half our global population within months.

They drove us slavishly to provide them with raw materials, minerals, plants and animals. As resistance quickly waned, members of our tribes were selected as go-betweens. They singled out our weakest males for this task, the first Primals to be taught the grating Andulakun language, a coarse contrast to our own melodious tongue.

The Andulakuns endowed these Primals with gifts and privileges, allotting them special living quarters. The wealth of these collaborators attracted more females to these inept specimens, a situation bound to fester male resentment. Fighting again erupted in our ranks. Naturally the Andulakuns armed the collaborators, but without the wider support of the majority, this initiative fortunately floundered.

The aliens also took particular interest in our women, especially the young girls around puberty and naturally our younger women, pregnant or otherwise. Females were routinely selected and returned weeks later, much changed in body and spirit: timid, subdued, melancholic. Our healers determined virgins had been ruined and mothers had given birth. Some had visible abdominal scars, but few retained the memory of their experiences. This continued for years. There are no words enough to describe our grief, our loss.

New Andulakuns gradually appeared more Primal looking, and not so foul smelling. After three hundred years, the original Andulakuns were like a myth, because those who ruled us were more a variation of a Primal, except for pigmentation and stature. Primals were musty with dark skins and natural hues from red to brown and stocky built, whilst Andulakun Elites remained tall with a purplish tinge. Only the most sensitive among us could now detect their diminished odour, rendered more rancid and sea-weedy with a camphorated hint, the trident markings on their foreheads now barely visible.

Male Andulakuns mainly amused themselves with our females, a few taking interest in our boys as well. They gleefully castrated our males for sport without any provocation. Their own females tended to stick to their own kind, only rarely being indulgent with a male Primal. Such unions were forbidden. A Primal man could be castrated or tortured for such an "attack". A simple execution never sufficed. Such were the sanctions governing our lives. By these designs, Elite women first appeared mysterious and inaccessible, festooned from head to toe with the refashioned stones and metals our men and women toiled to extract from the mines, some dying in the process. As time passed, many of our men become fixated with their women, paradoxically enough to die for. We did not then understand this was all part of a long-term strategy of assimilation.

Sustained "attacks" on our women produced the class of Socials, who had elevated status between us and the Elite. In some instances, Socials could be worse than Elites, being a particularly mean tempered, malicious breed: spoilt, flesh eaters. Our female mortality rate was initially high, with a large percent of stillborns. Others suffered deformities or strange illnesses. These rejects they used for analysis. Socials could only mate with each other but were destined to become the largest group in Andulakun society. We Primals were the Worker Class, the Socials the Administrative Class and the Elites the Ruling Class. Our life span quickly reduced to an average forty-five years from our original one hundred plus years.

Vast industrial cities were built and populated under Andulakun rule. Andulakun society flourished as the resources feeding their success steadily flowed, before plummeting with disastrous consequences. Our atmosphere became polluted, dull. Strange plants were cultivated, others modified. New animals were bred; vicious flesh eaters. There was nothing taboo to Andulakuns. They ate everything and indulged in anything that enhanced their peculiar enjoyment of our world, given to extreme excesses in all things. This was their heaven at our expense.

Elites had their own schools and the Socials theirs. History was written thus: Andulakuns were the first to inhabit our world and had genetically engineered Primals as a Worker Class. Andulakun science confirmed these facts. Primals were prohibited from recounting myths or stories to the contrary. The Primal language was likewise outlawed.

    The Sensitives among us made a pact against these prohibitions. Thus, secrecy helped to enhance our latent telepathic abilities and preserve some of our heritage. Without realising it, we began tapping into unknown depths and energies within our own evolving make-ups, despite their conditioning.

    Sensitive Primals did not readily adapt to Andulakun society. This may have facilitated the telepathic bonds between us to grow stronger. Though the Andulakuns suspected our ability, as it did not appear to pose a direct threat to them, it was dismissed as a primitive means of communication, but nonetheless declared subversive. What else had we Primals left? If they cut out our brains, what practical use would we really serve? For our part, we were only too pleased this characteristic was not genetically transferable. Andulakuns sharing their own private thoughts would surely lead to more anarchy than even they could stand.

    After five hundred years, the mating rules were suddenly relaxed. Elites were allowed to mate with Socials and Primals were gradually allowed to marry Socials, regardless of existing Primal partners. The lifestyle of the Socials was certainly more privileged than that of a Primal's, so Primals deserted their partners in droves for the first Social condescending an interest in them. These Primals dressed in the latest Andulakun fashion, even painting their skins purple. For a Primal, the only route to success in Andulakun society was to marry a Social. We did not fully appreciate that as with our planetary resources, our genes were a special commodity. Only the survivors would better understand why such a brutally advanced race, who first ravaged their minion captives, would later insist on progressively interbreeding with them, finally positively endorsing mixed relationships. Perhaps it is a simple universal fact that all life-forms are immortalised by passing their genes to the next generation.

Like a bird we called the bukcoo, Andulakuns laid their eggs in other birds' nests, using us to carry their progeny to inevitably obliterate our own kind. We were expendable, our value diminishing with time. The Elite woman was the final solution in their domination of us, for she had represented both the stick and the carrot. From practising a vague conservative sexuality, Andulakun society launched itself into a degenerate climax of sexual anarchy and debauchery. Whatever the current trend, Andulakuns revelled in promoting to the hilt. The freedom of sexual choice was now the order of the day. Anything went. It was a wonder any of us retained a semblance of our own sanity.

Patriotic Primals desperately clung to the remnants of our traditions, our identity, the last vestiges of self, praying to our Creators, even at the brink of what was increasingly looking like our imminent extinction. To the Andulakuns we were nothing more than amusing relics.

A thousand years had passed quickly, only a few hundred Primals survived, though our work admittedly over the years had long since eased with the introduction of machines. We were now a "Servant Class" exclusively for Elite families. They were our guardians.

It is said: "nothing lasts for ever".

Vast areas of land were agriculturally exhausted or polluted as the ecosystem destabilised. The threat of famine loomed. Rationing was ordered. The Andulakun solution was to simply produce synthetic food to supplement dietary requirements. This created an additional strain on Primals. Our stomachs were not as hardy as theirs. We would probably have succumbed to malnutrition and further diseases but for the first chink in their armour.

Chapter 2

"*A great darkness will precede the death of the first, who will be the last.*"

1st Primal Prophet

Xyla's master was now a civilian Elite, pursuing his love of architecture. All Elites were members of the military order, whether in active service or not. She was a Primal

Sensitive who served him as a housekeeper. Fortunately, unlike the days of old, this was not a live-in position. Xyla was always pleased to return to her own kind in the evenings, leaving the Andulakuns to entertain themselves, glad also to escape the focus of her master's overbearing wife. Once Primals had been their main source of entertainment, but as their needs were gradually supplemented, more challenging pursuits were cultivated for recreation.

Andulakuns at work tended to be quite disciplined. When at play, they were reckless as they were disciplined, delighting in physical combat of varying descriptions, to the death if need be. Pain was crucial to their survival; a celebration. Pain was enshrined and tastefully encapsulated in their daily imagery and rituals. To feel pain was to be alive: to inflict pain was a passion. The dangerous tightrope of pain and death tantalised and fascinated them.

Andulakuns had wrestling rings in their dens. An evening's entertainment could end with one of the guests needing serious medical attention. Remarkably this was only occasionally fatal. Death was sport.

Many a morning Xyla's day would commence with the scrubbing of dried blood, a task for which she wore special gloves and a mask, as direct contact with Andulakun blood was still toxic. How Primals were enabled to carry their offspring was a mystery to her people, suspecting this tolerance had something to do with the vaccination programme or that their food supply was laced with an anti-toxin.

Some masters delighted in making servants stay to watch these violent wrestling bouts, but fortunately Bugarn thought her presence would only inhibit matters.

Andulakuns loved to gather en masse. Thousands would visit weekly open air Bulletin Centres where continental news was broadcast in a civilised atmosphere. It was at one such session that they learnt of the inexplicable decline in the Andulakun birth-rate, with females increasingly prone to sterility. Additionally, a few Socials had reportedly given birth to Primals. This was easily explained by the fact that Primals had been marrying Socials. What they omitted to share was the fact that Socials who were not married to Primals were also producing Primals, infidelities notwithstanding. All such offspring were retained by the state for research. Surprisingly, not everyone was happy about this.

Later, rumours surfaced about Andulakun women also giving birth to Archetypes. To Bugarn's ears, all this signalled trouble. Times had changed, perhaps for the worst. The Socials had deliberately not been taught about Archetypes. Their understanding of their origins had been rewritten to facilitate a new breed on a new world. The very fabric of Andulakun society could be jeopardised. He needed more information, leaving the gathering early to contact a technician in biological research. Slank was a promising Social, the type seriously being considered for unprecedented entry into the lower echelons of the new Elite Order.

"Slank?"

"Captain Bugarn, Sir, I'm honoured."

"Relax Slank, I don't bite after breakfast."

"I'm sorry. How's your family Sir?"

"Pretty good. My son is walking now."

"Oh really?! Children grow up so fast these days."

"They certainly do. As a matter of fact, that's what I called about. What's the latest on these birth anomalies?"

"Oh scarn, I'm not supposed …"

"It's okay, I'm tapping in a code for a secure channel - go ahead."

"Verified and cleared Sir. Well, in simple terms, what we've got here are some major translocation problems. We're really not sure why. Genetic mayhem with all kinds of mutations happening; Socials dying in labour. It's worse than the reports."

"Iron and clay."

"Pardon Sir?"

"Just some Primal mumbo jumbo I came across. When did it start?"

"Can't say for sure but maybe six months ago. We've got our best people working on it, sequencing machines working overtime."

"What about these Primals the Socials are having? They for real? You sure they're not the result of some extracurricular Primal hanky panky?"

"No, they're definitely mutations. Phenotype on the outside only, not your average Primal genotype."

"Next generation?"

"Could be, only without us engineering them. Nature did this one all by herself. We suspect Socials may have been dumping them for years in Primal areas because of the stigma of attachment. There may be many more out there. We just didn't pick up what was going on sooner."

He confirmed an increasing number of Archetypes were also being born, and there was nothing they could presently do to stop that either. The Ancients, after all, had simply switched off certain genes, not deleted them. Their usefulness in other environments could prove critical for the next invasion.

An announcement was due regarding all remaining Primals. They too would be declared a natural resource. Slank didn't know why it hadn't been done sooner. Perhaps this calamity could have been avoided.

Bugarn thanked him and drove home. He wondered how Xyla would cope in a secure unit. Though Primals enjoyed a degree of freedom, pushed too hard, Andulakun contingency plans could quickly make their situation more difficult. This needed to be handled with special care. He knew the more militaristic of the Elite Order were not known for their delicacy. He'd seek an urgent appointment with his old Commander.

Xyla arrived home. The rumours had reached her compound as well. A special meeting was in progress. Fear and apprehension pervaded the atmosphere. A few Primals who had mated with Andulakun women were also back in the fold. The military was searching for them. These men were in shock. Their wives had gone into premature labour which they had had to assist with as trained, there being no time to call a medic. They had never seen such creatures amongst their own people. Aghast that the legends were true, they had run vomiting from the scenes.

The Elder Primal, a female, called the meeting to order. A blessing was said to the Great One Spirit.

She reminded them that as a people, since the time of The Invasion, they had walked in fear but survived Andulakun domination while many species had disappeared. Someone shouted that their own fate was still in the balance. She wearily nodded acknowledgement of this truth.

She began, "I have the unenviable task of preparing you for the future. I cannot hide what I have seen in the mind's eye, because soon, as they did in the past, the Andulakuns will come to round us all up."

"But why?" some shouted. What have we done?!"

"Done?" she sighed, "You exist. In their attempt to cover up their own historical lies, and in order to perpetuate their own alien breed, they will seek to repair the damage and attempt to further use us to reinvent themselves. Without us, they will simply stare in the face of their own doom."

The meeting disintegrated into an uproar. The Second shouted for order. Someone asked if there was nothing they could do to resist them. The Elder replied that she had painstakingly held their traditions together, through great difficulties. The only defence she felt they had was the thought merger: one mind, one vibration. The true Creators would answer. As for the Andulakuns, again, the Primals themselves would be key to the solution. Some Primals had little confidence in this passive inaction. After all, hadn't the Creators allowed their neigh annihilation in the face of this pernicious evil?

"We could fight back, launch an attack," a youngster demonstrated with his fist.

"Do that and you will certainly be throwing your life away to the enemy's cause," she reproached. "There are too few of us to waste our lives on useless exercises. No, it is time for us to start believing in our own abilities and not those of the Andulakuns. We are only helpless if we lose ourselves completely to them. We must prepare. Come, let us join in the great wonder of minds which our ancestors taught."

A few non-Sensitives left, denouncing the Elder's willingness to do nothing other than meditate on their predicament.

It didn't take long for a change of mood to descend on those remaining, the Elder being expert in calming nerves. Xyla thoroughly enjoyed merge sessions. They left her feeling revitalised. Sometimes she felt her very thoughts leave her body, touching those of the ancestors ... and others ... thought forms she could not place. Once she sensed she could almost touch the Great One Spirit, but told herself that could not be. The Great One Spirit would hardly notice an insignificant Primal like herself. She too wrestled with the question of why the true Creators, if all the legends were to be believed, had allowed these terrible aliens to destroy her world, her race, reducing them to their pathetic existence. When these thoughts emerged, she intensely felt the presence of the Elder in rebuke, or perhaps she only imagined this, and would quickly divert her thoughts to more productive inclinations.

At the end of the session the Elder asked her to stay.

"Xyla," she touched the young woman's face, "you are purer in heart than most here and for a young woman still unmarried, though admittedly we are few in number."

"… I, I …"

"Hush child. It has all been for the good."

"It's not that I don't want to marry Elder. The women can squabble so. Somehow it just doesn't seem right for me. Now it all appears to be … academic."

The Elder sighed. "Yes, once we were monogamous, but polygamy in these times has helped to preserve the race as the men have been few in mind as well as body. You are housekeeper of far more than you imagine Xyla. It is your master who will discover who the true ruler of his household is. Be a guide to him and in so doing help your people survive this bitter end."

"Me?" she asked bemused. "What could I possibly do?"

"Nothing more than what comes natural to you. When the time comes, you will know." She patted her lap. Xyla left confused that the Elder should have singled her out.

Chapter 3

Bugarn was successful in being granted an appointment with his Commander, who was genuinely pleased to see him. After they reminisced about the old days, Bugarn came to the point as was his way.

"Forgive me," the Commander interrupted, "I know we have made many changes since The Invasion, and we are accustomed to now caring for these Primals, but our actions are always dictated by how best Primals can serve our cause."

Bugarn agreed, but reminded him of how the Ancients had over zealously killed thousands of Primals due to their heavy handed control of the situation, with countless more dying during the experimental years. If Andulakuns needed the few Primals that were left to be of any long-term benefit – not just to avert the immediate crisis, he urged a kinder approach, bar putting them in complete stasis. Reducing them back to the status of lab rats was surely not the way to end it all, even though he knew such had been the outcome on other worlds.

"I take on board what you're saying Bugarn. There is much merit in it, but I'm afraid the order has already been issued to bring them in. Now, I know you have a personal interest in one of them, er Xyla is it?"

Bugarn confirmed this, even though he knew the Commander to be certain.

"I'll make arrangements for you to visit this Primal in a few weeks. Till then, we'll see how it goes."

He left the office, uncertain as to what had really driven him thus far. Anyway, it was done. The seed had been planted. He could kick himself. He could have had Xyla to himself if he had just taken her. Yet that would never have been enough for him. He needed her to surrender unconditionally to him without fear, to possess her body and soul. His wife was not oblivious to his dilemma, mocking him about it. It was she who insisted Xyla should clean up the blood in the old way after the fights, just to rub his nose in her discomfort.

Why was he constantly filled with concern for this Primal? Was his character flawed by admiring that most disarming weakness in her … her innocence?

The unit deployed in the early hours, as was their tendency. The blue uniformed Tukbun kicked down doors, smashed everything that was breakable and aggressively dragged Primals from their beds.

Two weeks later, Bugarn was given leave to visit Xyla as the Commander had promised. He was visibly shocked when he saw her. She was drawn and noticeably tired, her hair a matted mess. Even so, he could tell her gentle spirit was holding.

"Xyla, is there anything you would like me to do for you?" he almost pleaded across the table. "Anything?"

She thought carefully about the question, at the last moment remembering what the Elder had said.

"They keep us apart you know, but they can never split us up. We haven't been outside since we were brought here. Almost every day they take samples of blood. Yet they feed us this tasteless substance …" she trailed off.

"I promise you, I'll do the best I can, you must believe that." He wanted to reach for her hand, but even now feared rejection.

"I kept a window box at the back of our compound. We salvaged seeds your people threw away, growing plants for food, flowers too, even though it was forbidden.

I marvelled at the simple resilience of life, with nothing more than air, water and the soil. What else did they need besides a little care?"

He stared at her. She didn't return his gaze. She simply rose slowly and left, oblivious to his agony.

It took several weeks, but the food was finally changed to the most natural they could offer, causing a dramatic improvement in Primal psychological and physical condition. Daily exercise periods were added. The joy of being able to see each other even under restrictions was ecstatic. Xyla wondered if it had indeed been Bugarn's doing. Primals had become the most precious commodity to the Andulakuns.

Socials now treasured the Primal children they sporadically bore, becoming incensed when they were confiscated. Bugarn's fears were all too soon realised. It was not long before Andulakun society disintegrated into discernible civil war. He was recalled into active service, promoted to Chief Peace Mediator. Primals were to be the prize at the end of this internecine struggle. Xyla could still be his greatest trophy. Too late, his desire for her exclusive attention might not be fully realised in the long-term scheme of things.

On the day of the Great Eclipse, with the sun approaching its peak cyclic activity, the Andulakun capital was besieged by rebels. Guards around the detention centre had been fortified. All over the continent underground tremors rumbled, the heavens growing angry with huge storm systems forming, creating violent tornadoes, which ripped across city after city. As the day progressed, the continent erupted as the Mother Essence spewed burning magma and ash.

The Elder signalled the mind merge. Though separated by walls and steel frames, it was to be the most exhilarating of experiences. Thick choking darkness enveloped the warring parties, forcing them to cease hostilities. As the sun slowly emerged from the shadow of the moon, renewed energy channelled through the walls and floors of the holding building. Xyla opened her eyes to see actual streaks of white light flowing towards her. The building was bathed in this increasing swirl. The light stung the confused Andulakuns, who did not know what was happening. They fled in pain, leaving the Primals to their fate.

They tried firing pulses at the building to dispel the energy but found their weapons were inoperable. In frustration the Commander instructed Bugarn to order an aerial assault. Communications were severely disrupted by the atmospheric disturbances. When they finally connected, the answer from base control was negative, nothing could get airborne due to tornado and quake activity, as many of their flying machines had been destroyed on the ground.

"What the blazes does he think he's doing?" Bugarn cried, spotting Slank running in the direction of the building with a small child in his arms. He called out but Slank didn't respond, disappearing into the swirl.

There was further commotion, as more Socials broke cover, also running to the building, again, some of them carrying children. Attempts made to restrain them resulted in an intense electrical discharge throwing their would be restrainers to the ground, preventing physical contact.

They headed for the large conference hall. Here Primals were already gathered; men and women cradling babies and toddlers. No words were spoken. The energy stripped the Andulakun disguise, revealing the runners too were in fact next level Primals, who had been passing for years as Socials, injecting themselves with pigment and applying markings. Some had been dumped in Primal areas as babies, the Primals raising them as their own with their meagre resources. A few had been raised in disguise by conscientious Social parents, who simply did not want their child to be discriminated against because he or she was different. These so called Primos were also telepaths, all having learnt the way of the merge and had received guidance from the Elder over the years, on a few occasions meeting secretly. All had been compelled to the area for the Eclipse. Slank was right; they were indeed next generation Primals, the Mother Essence having reasserted her authority over Andulakun tampering with her creation, gleaning even this remnant back from the tide of alien seeds, endowing them with new abilities.

The energy vortex around the building intensified, forcing the Andulakuns further back. The anticlockwise swirl was spectacular, now spiralling so fast the building was totally engulfed.

At last the wind dropped and the tremors subsided. Bugarn wiped a clump of dirt from his eyes, raising his head to find the vortex had vanished along with the building.

"What in the name of the stars happened here?" the Commander spurted out.

"I think our charges were just harvested from us Sir," Bugarn deduced.

"What?! But by whom?"

"I'm not sure, but by the looks of things, maybe it's time we too moved on from this world."

"I'll be damned if there's anything of value to keep us here anymore, except the obvious fact that we don't appear to have enough energy to enable the escape velocity of a fly!"

Bugarn couldn't help thinking this was some kind of natural justice. For the first time it was the Andulakuns who stood staring into oblivion, marooned on a depleted planet.

The tremors trebled their intensity.

MOTHER EARTH

If I could but restore her face,
If I could but restore her grace;
She would so evergreen remain
With comely seas abundant with fish
And clear blue skies with air afresh,
And creatures who'd tend her every wish
For all to live to know her charms -
If I could keep her safe from harm.

AFTER THE AFTERMATH

If I could but restore her face …

She sat within despair itself,
This young woman, withered dry as a leaf: a living tomb.
She sat, her head betwixt her knees, wailing such harrowing sounds
That pierced the very essence of one's being
And ripped a place in one's soul.

Feeling his shadow, she raised her cotton-white head.
And he looked down into those dark absorbent craters;
Along ridges of encrusted pain;
Through charred fissures where tears once burned their course then dried.

And the young man asked aloof, "Mother Earth, why must you weep so?"
"I weep for my children and for my dreams," she replied.
"Why so?" he returned, haughtily, so proud,
The sun arrayed behind him,
His black cloak fluttering on a wind stench of death.
"I am alone here," the woman said, "the children are hungry, cold, naked …
My dream is for the strength to feed and clothe them."

He stared at her, this cataclysm of disaster personified,
And knew her well, yet still he knew her not.
She gazed back at him, even through her blindness and asked:
"You have no child?"
"No!" The response was defiantly indignant.
"Ah," she soothed, "but I see your issues yet.
Your child is power and your dream glory.
I would cry a deluge for you but you have bled me so."

"These breasts," she stroked the shrivelled sacks,

"Once bore sweet nutrients of life – gone sour.

Yet the children still suckle there, I have nought else to give them.

These fingers, "she raised the fragile appendages

Where skin bared bones like worn out gloves,

"Used to nimbly sow seeds, tend bees, shear sheep; all rotted to dust."

She drew breath and gasped.

"Yes it is you! O Arrogance, did I not feed you?!

Hate, did I note love you?

Greed, did I not clothe you?

O War, did I not bear you?"

"Bitch! Whore!" he bawled,

And would have swallowed his filthy crippled mother whole,

But she held him fast with a craggy smile.

"My heart is well pleased to have you so near O Son," she calmed.

"Who now is left to herald your victory?

No captive here for you to oppress?

No land to glorify your eyes?

You murdered all that fuelled your lust,

And the rest with me today shall die in one breath.

But you another day must see to say: 'I War at length did win the day,'
And eat The Aftermath alone …"

If I could but restore her face …

A COMPLICATED LOVE

(Phone rings, he answers)

"Hey, my main man.
Where you been?
What's that? Repeat that …
Oh so you're in love now. You are?!
No wonder I ain't been hearing from you.
So who is she, this woman who's captured your heart?
It's complicated?
What she married?
No?
Got a bunch of kids and an ex-husband?
Oh all out the picture …
Ahh huh.
She a boxer or something?
No huh. Long as she don't do none a that martial arts stuff.
Got to watch out for them gals now.
Oh you don't think so. Good. Good.
So what's up?
It a distant thing?

She live in Alaska or somewhere remote like that?
Darkest Peru or some such place?
Oh that's a bit of an issue then.
Yeh, I can see how that could cause some problems.
Ok so what else?
She a person of small stature to be politically correct?
I know you go for them quirky women sometimes.
She an amputee?
No?
Got too many tattoos and piercings even for you maybe?
No?
She a Goth, funny spiky hair thing?
Uh, uhhh?
Well, hey … I'm running out of ideas here.
Help me out.
What's that?
Ah, she's a religious fruit cake.
You got me there …
Anything else?
She's what?
Religious and black?
Oh you got to be kidding me!
Aren't your folks Italian/Russian?
Russian and Italian – yeh I know you were adopted.
You tell her?

You haven't spoken to her about it?

Er, you haven't spoken to her at all?!

Are you kidding me?

I know you love to play Russian roulette but this …

She live in Timbuktu or something?

They got computers out there yet?

Come to think of it, they even got mobiles?

It gets worse …

How much worse can this get?

You've never seen her?!

You telling me you're all broke up

About some religious black chick you've never met?

You're in love with Ms Tropical Scotch Mist Never Show?!

Remember when you had that accident?

Yeh, fell upside your head …

Better ask your doctor to look at that X-ray again.

Call me back after you've seen him.

I'm here for you man …

Just you remember that …

Got your back always …"

(Hangs up the phone - mumbles)

"Crazy son of a whatnot …"

(Calls him back later ...)

"Hey man, sorry I went off on you like that.
I was thinking …
You afraid she might learn your secret?
What's that? You think she already knows …
How could she possibly?
Oh one of them rare savvy types …
Ah huh … Well, go get your wings clipped or something.
I heard that!
Nah don't call Stupid Cupid whatever you do!
Probably got you in this mess in the first darn place ...
Got your back man, always remember …"

THE END OF THE HUNT

She was fully clothed and much more to his eminent dissatisfaction, a terrific understatement under the circumstances. She stood approximately 8 metres away from him, the closest they had been in forty thousand years; a blink of an eye to their kind.

"So why did you run?"

"Perhaps it was the lure of the galactic plane passing. How do I know Unix?" She shook her head and shrugged her shoulders, looked at him wide-eyed.

"Don't mock me Ishell. I am weary from hunting you and I find you ingloriously playing lover to this human species when you could have been with me all this time. I would have expected such a flight of fancy from others of our kind, but you, it took me by surprise." He laughed. "Your father hid this event from me, for he certainly knew."

"I am his daughter and he had the right Sir."

"You dare talk to me, your husband, of rights my Lady?"

"I ..."

"I will not hear it and you will not speak it – do I make myself clear?" He was angry.

"Clear as a Tyrant, perhaps I ran because of the things I know you do. Things you will repent. I have seen it."

"You know nothing of the things I do and why I have to do them. Perhaps you should ask your father about that. I'll have no more of this. Remove that ridiculous camouflage you're wearing and come to me."

"He continued: "Did they find the lock within you, these humans?" He looked down at his feet for the first time and back at her.

"No Sir, they surely did not." He nodded with knowing satisfaction as he knew them to be incapable of such.

She made to speak again but he shouted: "Now, I said remove the camouflage." The garments dropped and the rest melted in a pool around her feet, before draining away. She left herself the slightest undergarments which showed through a full-length gossamer dress, where raindrops hung suspended and glistening. Her aroma seeded and saturated the dwindling space between them by the second.

"Lose the undergarments but keep the dress and come to me …" He beckoned her.

She did obey. There was an inevitability about it that now excited her and he was certainly tired of her playing games.

She stood before him and they looked each other in the eyes. He breathed, she breathed. He raised his hand to her formation of breasts in human terms; his hands were cold from the frustrating chill of forty thousand years of waiting. Her breasts rose and her nipples tingled, stirring sensations in her abdomen and between her legs.

"No more games he whispered." He brushed through the flimsy gossamer and gently pulled her close to his lips. His first relief came as she tasted of black ripened cherries. She straight responded by opening her mouth and he did enter and mingle with her tongue.

Her garments melted and he whispered again in her ear that she should spread her legs as he held her lower back and she wrapped one leg around his, allowing him to slip announced into her domain … Ishell fervently caressed her husband. They stayed entangled so for twenty-four of your Earth hours, dissolving into an ionic storm which in time emerged as an embryonic nebula, created by an unfurling sigh and a scream that reverberated as a spatial anomaly.

When he was thoroughly sated, he finally rose. "Duty calls, I must go now. I want you to birth our child within the next twenty-four hours."

"Twenty-four hours?! It normally takes at least three days."

"I said no more games Ishell; I know full well what you are capable of when you put your mind to it. I want our first child birthed within the next twenty-four hours and you will not leave the confines of this place until you do. I will send attendants to you."

She had not been prepared for this. No honeymoon even! To be confined straightaway into motherhood.

"The rest you can have during the course of the month so you'll be very busy. Manifestly, responsibilities enough to stem any more notions of gallivanting across the universe, away from home. And I forbid you telling our children any of your stories about those times." She laid there stunned, but on reflection, glad she had grasped the opportunity to travel when she had before settling down for all time.

The attendants arrived with trays of delicacies as she was famished enough to eat a mountain dusted with iridium: choice fruits with frosted snowflakes; finger food with the finest grains of gold and iron; hydro-helium laced with spices and the purest water in the universe.

"I need roses," she called after him. "Lots of lovely roses," pleading.

He snapped his fingers and a pond loaded tub appeared. She bathed in the silky smooth petals, washing her hair and polishing her skin with fragrance.

Her belly popped. The baby was growing rapidly of course. She shed a tear. She did love him ... What's forty thousand years to be sure for goodness sake?!

THE TICKLED BIRD

(Part 1)

When he later remembered, it had been a night of a supermoon. Julian had followed her into the car park of a pub called *The Tickled Bird*. He was certain when she had entered her vehicle, she had been wearing a dark grey suit. Under the light of this moon it seemed more green than grey. Perhaps the nearby street lights also added to the effect.

He trailed in the wake of her sleek compact body. She headed straight for the ladies room. He approached the bar, ordered a stout on draught. The pub had an old 1920's feel which took him back to those black and white movie scenes. Funny how he'd never spotted the place before, though he had driven around the area on numerous occasions. He wouldn't have missed it. He was certain. Julian tapped his temple, a habit of his when he'd lost something.

The scrawl on the blackboard announced they were serving rhubarb crumble for dessert. He glanced back at the ladies room and to the clock on the wall. She was taking her time. Probably thought the bloke would be worth it. He knew better of course.

He hadn't eaten a good rhubarb crumble since his grandmother passed away. He ordered some, without custard and scanned for a seat. He paid for the dessert. Half-way on his beeline for a table, the lights dimmed. He sat down as music started pounding that big band ragtime sound. A bunch of bounding dancers appeared in the funnel of a huge spotlight, all dressed in black and white stripes with chess piece headdresses. It was surreal. He dropped his spoon of rhubarb, had a swig of stout instead. They wriggled and pranced around to the beat on the square patch: syncopated animal moves; mixed black bottom rooted ragtime. Then as suddenly as the performance had erupted, it likewise ended. The lights slammed on and he hadn't even noticed when the dancers left.

She was sat at a table directly opposite him but when he turned to acknowledge the presence of the person standing next to him, she was also there. Julian wasn't easily spooked. She obviously couldn't be in two places at once, unless she had a twin he didn't know about. Maybe the other woman was some sort of decoy?

"Mr Mann, I see you were a touch distracted there."

"Ahh, Miss Green. I hadn't realised you'd noticed me. Obviously more going on here than I imagined. Why don't you have a seat? You seem to have me at a disadvantage presently. Can I get you a drink?" This could provide him with an opportunity to take a closer look at the other woman. He stood up, meeting her height and slant almond brown eyes.

"You know Mr Mann, you've put yourself through an awful lot of trouble to just offer me a drink," spoken with complete control.

"Could be you're the kind of trouble worth finding Miss Green. Please, have a seat. We can both keep an eye out for your friend."

"Tut, tut. You're so presumptuous Mr Mann." She wagged a verdant polished finger. "Whatever made you think I'm meeting a friend here?" tilting her head but holding her piercing gaze. Julian raised both eyebrows. He twisted the ring on his little finger, idling over his mistake. It was time for him to raise his game. She turned and walked away before he could say another word.

(Part 2)

Julian decided to take his report to R&P himself. It was a glorious late spring day. He fancied he might even catch a hint of a tan on his walk via the park.

He loosened his tie, undid his top shirt buttons to afford himself a sense of freedom. He always wore a tie in his line of business, as he never quite knew where he might end up.

She breezed past him. He halted dead in his tracks, looked around. He saw that she too had stopped and was looking back at him from under the brim of a large straw hat. They instinctively walked back towards each other, meeting in the middle of the path, the dots on her 50's style polka dress rolling with each step, her waist tied with a broad black leather belt.

She generously held out a hand.

"Why, Mr Mann, we meet again." Julian stuffed the envelope under his armpit, eagerly shook her hand with both of his, feeling for her pulse. She pretended she hadn't noticed. Miss Green's beat felt every bit as healthy as her appearance. A springtime surge pulsed through his body. He retrieved his hand before he embarrassed himself, adjusting the envelope to assist his grip on the situation. She obliged by readjusting her hat while treating him with a knowing grin. This had the effect of instantly making him feel like a fisherman being reeled out of the sea by the catch of the month.

He pulled out a business card and handed it to her.

"I'm ever so sorry Miss Green, but I'm on an errand just now. Please."

"Oh?" she regarded the card, tapped it on her palm.

"Yes. But do give me a ring late afternoon."

"You know, I'm beginning to find you quite amusing Mr Mann. I'll ring you at 6:00 PM. Don't work too hard or you'll have no energy left for any fun and that would be such a pity."

He was wondering how to respond but she was already five metres away. Julian glanced at his polished shoes, looking up in time to see her vanish around some bushes in budding orange bloom.

He felt hot, bothered and a touch jaded. He hurried to the water fountain, had a drink and dabbed his face. He didn't know what had come over him.

Reid & Pinnacle was based a few streets away in a multi-occupied ten storey grey block. He pushed the heavy glass door, walking up six steps to the reception desk behind a man with a briefcase. About the only things to break the monotony of grey speckled walls in the lobby was a vase with six large lilies to the left of the receptionist who wore a dark blue suit. While he waited, all four lifts arrived in a full sweep, to the bell of their red stop lights. Julian couldn't but notice the people exiting the lifts. He observed their faces were ripe red as a suit of jack of diamonds; recalling, blackjack was a game he never learned to play for some strange reason. The receptionist called next, efficiently having her hand out for the envelope. Before he could even speak, she turned a pad and pointed to where he should sign.

"Just there please." Her tone was brusque and her badge read Ms H Singer. She called Mr Roper's office to let them know an urgent document had arrived. Julian thought she could probably lead a dirge. The envelope's contents were encoded in such a way as not to clearly identify the subject and in any case labelled for the addressee only. She tore him a receipt, ushering the next person to approach. No doubt Roper would be in touch if anything more was required.

On clearing the last step, the lifts sounded their arrival again so much louder. Julian glanced back as the doors opened and the large triangular green light lit up. No one came out. And why should they? The thought flitted to the back of his mind as he pushed his way out.

Back in his box office, the phone rang.

"Mr Mann?"

"Miss Green."

"Mr Mann, I have a story for you." It was his turn to say:

"Oh? Would you like to meet up somewhere?"

"I'd like that very much. How about 9:30 PM?"

"That's good for me. Ah where?"

"Oh you know where Mr Mann. Think you can find it again?"

"I'm sure I will if you want me to Miss Green. The Tickled Bird at 9.30 PM and I'll be all ears."

She hung up.

(Part 3)

Julian had no trouble finding The Tickled Bird again. Still feeling queasy from earlier in the day, he hadn't eaten anything since. He chose to sit in the same place as it was free and would make it easy for her to spot him. The pub was as busy as before. He watched her approach. Why she chose to wear a suit in that atmosphere he found intriguing, yet oddly enough it really didn't come across as out of place there. She definitely reminded him of someone. He just couldn't place her.

She had a drink in her hand. She placed it on the table, pushing it towards him.

"Drink this. It's only water with a slice of squeezed lemon. You look as if you need something simple and refreshing."

"Thank you." He took a sip purely on trust. "Remembered I hadn't eaten all day."

"Well I wouldn't do anything about that now. Sometimes the body needs a rest and tries to warn."

"If you say so. Cheers." He took another sip.

"You said you had a story to tell me."

"In a moment Mr Mann." Julian had a sudden urge to run to the gents.

"Excuse me."

"Part of the cleansing process Mr Mann. You'll find the gents ahead of you and first left."

When he got back he was indeed looking and feeling refreshed. She didn't wait for him to be seated.

"I know you think you understand the rules the people who hired you play by, but they will never tell you what this is in fact all about. The longer they retain you, the worst things will become. While you may have some allegiance to them for reasons again that you don't really understand, I assure you Mr Mann your soul is in the balance here."

"My soul? My dear Miss Green, I have a body to feed, one almost ex-wife and two children to support. Oh and not to forget a recently acquired cat. In this PI business, I'm very well paid for flexible hours. What could be simpler in a downturn?"

The pub was changing. A light emanated from the ceiling and Miss Green herself was radiating in front of him. The whole place was engulfed by a rainbow sequence of blinding lights, while Miss Green shone green and white. The silence was clammy, almost deafening as if there should have been sound accompaniment as before. Everyone was staring at him.

He was relieved to wake up in a cold sweat. He gasped, just laid there totally drenched before throwing off the duvet. He rubbed his eyes, ruffled his hair.

"Bloody nightmare." Perhaps he was coming down with something. Loss of appetite …

It was 9:30 AM. He could do with a strong coffee, Blue Mountain preferably. He put the kettle on before making his way downstairs to collect the post. There was more than the usual amount and a couple copies of the local paper. When he checked one local front page it read 19th May. But that had been two weeks prior. He'd picked up his post and papers before then, been in and out of the flat. This had to be a print error. He checked the other weekly papers, but these too were so dated. He ran up the stairs and turned on the TV, the date stated 19th May. He rummaged through the mail, finding a letter from Reid & Pinnacle. It was a remittance for work completed, the money having been paid directly into his account.

While he was trying to figure out what was going on, his attention was drawn to the breaking news on the TV, concerning a dramatic incident unfolding in Central London at the offices of Reid and Pinnacle. A female reporter was explaining how staff had had to evacuate the building, access to which had been cordoned off. The report was that the Chairman of the company, having called an extraordinary meeting, had locked the meeting room door and by some accounts had executed everyone inside after which he had committed suicide. The alarm had rung out when blood from one of the victims was seen seeping under the door of the polished stone floor. The unfolding story centred on a client's alleged report of massive fraud and mismanagement by the international company.

Julian folded on his leather chair in complete shock, as if he'd been hit by a juggernaut. His head felt like someone had cracked open his skull and scrambled his brain; spliced his life. It was some time before he realised his landline phone was ringing. Coming to, he tripped over his slippers, missing the call. Jolted back to current existence, he automatically played back the messages. Verona was reminding him to pick up the children by lunchtime; they were looking forward to it. Another was from Lionel wanting to meet up for drinks. The last message was from Miss Green. She thanked him for assisting her with their mutual problem, and that now that the *papier mâché* game had changed, she hoped he would find himself recovered enough to enjoy the rest of his day with his children despite the news.

Einstein, his new cat, pushed the door, eyes asking what was for breakfast. With all the recent excitement, Julian had forgotten to buy any shopping and the children would be staying for the weekend. His priorities had suddenly changed; his family came first. Einstein looked up at him, approving.

OUT IN THE COLD

You hear a baby scream
It pierces the night
He turns and says dim the light
It's too dark to see what's bothering me

Now you're awake got out of bed
It's snowing outside
Might as well make another pillow for your head
Share with crystals instead

You can hear him breathing as he travels east
Treads through your dreams, so comfortably
A snow leopard, better company
Treks through the night
As you climb through the light of the stars
No one knows where you are

Through the mist, one gaze
One never saw through the haze
Of what you believe is true
Mystifying, cruel …

THE GALLERY OF LIFE

Ella found herself in a room full of black and white pictures taken around the 1950's. She guessed the images were from across the West Indies. It was confusing, uncertain as she was about how she had come to be in the gallery. However, the photos captivated her interest, drawing her to speculate on whether she recognised anything.

There were scenes of people working in cane fields, women carrying loads on their heads, children bathing in a cove, fishermen: one of alligators thrashing their tails in a river, sweeping up a spray of water. As she moved along the elongated room, the images gradually phased into colour and became more vivid, alive; whispering tantalising secrets locked in the portrayal of tones, hidden in full view.

She halted before one exhibiting a Jonkonnu in explosive colourful progress. A man on stilts wore the head of an alligator and sporting a red bow tie while smoking a large cigar. Panning across from him was a lady dressed in a powder blue suit and framed sunglasses. The image held Ella's eye. She shifted uneasily to the next picture which depicted near enough the same scene. On closer inspection, the woman was in fact holding a little girl's hand. As she studied the scene, she recognised the woman to be none other than her own mother and the child, herself. This realisation was a shock. She gasped: froze.

The date on the caption read '21 December 1959'. The events of that day floated back to memory. It had been sweltering hot. Her mother had worn that Irish linen suit, carrying a white handbag and a fan. They had stopped for a while to watch the Jonkonnu; people singing, prancing to thumping drums and rasping horns. Another woman approached them who looked exactly like her mother but wearing one of her other suits, more fitted and contrastingly peachy. Without any exchange of words, her mother handed her to this new lady. The woman had grasped her firmly by the hand and proceeded to mill through the excited crowd. Ella had strained to see where her original mother went but quickly lost sight of her.

They finally stopped at a large department store on King Street, one with a moving Santa in the window, his mouth opening and closing very slowly: "Ho, ho, ho". Though fascinated by the striking figure, Ella had a distinct feeling he was unfriendly, finding comfort in the shield of glass between them. She had been relieved when her new mother pulled her away to buy something in another store because they gave away free calendars with purchases.

The scene receded in her mind. Someone was behind her. She turned to see a tall, bald and ghastly pale, grey-eyed man. He had a slit for a mouth, slits for ears and large hands. For all this he somehow looked rather familiar, as if his face was a template ready for an artist to etch features on.

"I see you're waking." He stared into the picture, barely moving his mouth.

Ella was surprised not to feel startled by his presence. She calmly responded, "I'm sure I've seen you before." He made no attempt to indulge her query.

"Where am I? What am I doing here?" turning to directly face him, that lost childlike curiosity lingering from the former images.

"All in good time. I can assure you, I'm here to help."

"Why should I need help? Am I in some sort of trouble?" It was hard to feel too anxious, as bizarre as this situation evidently was. It felt distinctly like she was dreaming.

"You're likely to be a little confused. Hardly surprising."

"An understatement under circumstances I'm not at all entirely sure of." The sense of being adult again was returning. She cleared her throat. "Yes I feel confused. I don't know how you fit into this crazy situation I find myself in, but if you truly want to help, perhaps you could start by telling me where I am and how I came to be here. I can't seem to remember what happened before finding myself here."

"That is probably the most confusing place of all to start, if you don't mind my saying," he replied unmoved. You may find it useful for the time being to simply finish looking at the paintings and photographs. There are a few more rooms to go. The final images should bring you up to speed."

"Is there anyone else here? Or are we alone?" She asked without any notion as to why.

"No one else will disturb you. The gallery is yours alone for this session." He exited before she could press him further.

For a second she thought perhaps she should have quizzed him more but was strangely also content that she hadn't. If that picture depicted two mothers as she remembered, then who was the second woman? Her mother did not have a twin and her other sisters bore only a slight resemblance.

Ella moved on to discover more key depictions of events in her life. Some brought smiles while others tapped tears. There was the first time she fell from a swing for example; her first school photo; seeing her father again before he died. Moving forward, pictures from when she first met Dane and later ones of their wedding day. She touched the last of these images and it came to life, again the shock of it. It had been a happy day. Wendy was there too. Recalling Wendy's presence had the effect of jolting Ella's disturbed memory of what had happened before her arrival at the gallery.

She was in the late stages of her first pregnancy but had been arguing with Dane. He had left his phone at home and she had answered it. A message had been left by someone listed as Robyn. For some reason she decided to listen to it in case it was something important. The voice she recognised instantly to be Wendy's, apologising for not calling him back. She went on in a contrite tone, "Dane, darling". A wave of fear had run through Ella's body, forcing her to grip her unsettled belly to steady herself. Breathing heavily, she lowered into an armchair, rubbing her belly. The baby had stirred, upset. She trawled through Dane's text messages and read another sent by "Robyn".

"Press Me

Hypnotic eyes
Piercing every inch of me
Drum beats, heart pumping
Press, you press me
Merlot running sticky
We flow in rhythmic warm embrace
Tongues lap defining moist edges
The beginning of you
The end of me

Press, you press me
Before we evaporate
Salty ... spent ..."

The message ended with: "That's how I feel when we're together ... Smile."

Ella had confronted Dane with the details of his betrayal that night. He initially tried to deny it. Wendy had been one of her closest friends since school days. How could he, how could they? Had the pregnancy made her so grotesque to him or had the affair started long before that? The next thing she knew, her waters had broken and an ambulance later arrived. That was the last thing she recalled as the final picture depicted. Ella instinctively reached for her belly but was horrified to discover there was no bump.

The guide returned.

"Where's my baby?! What's happened?" she asked frantic.

"Calm down. That's what you're here to decide. A rare opportunity has arisen as chance would have it, as far as this process goes in any event. You see, you've consistently shown great promise."

"Promise? Will you stop talking in riddles, please! What's happened to my baby? What's happened to him?" she pleaded, tears streaming.

The guide remained impassive. He acknowledged she had much to be angry about, but right then and there only decisions were of any importance. The final frames had yet to be filled. Nothing could be determined until then.

She fought back the tears in a desperate attempt to keep up with what he was saying through the torrent of emotions that had been evoked.

He explained there were two vectors ahead. She hadn't noticed them before. One of the nebulous vectors swirled blue, the other white. The options were explained. If she went through the blue vector, she would return to life but her son would die. If she chose the white vector, her son would survive but she would cease to be human.

"What does that mean? To cease to be human? Would I be simply dead or what?"

"The white option simply leads into the unknown." That was all he could tell her.

He left her to ponder; alone, tearful and distraught, gripped with grief and dire emptiness. The word 'unknown' began ringing in her head. She had no idea how long she remained in this state without the need for food or water. At no time did the guide reappear. With only the empty picture frames for company, all the other accesses had vanished. Tentatively she approached the vectors. The decision though impossible was nonetheless loaded, set in the past. The future lay ahead.

She stretched out her hand to the vector in front of her. Behind, the pictures on the wall began rapidly filling up. She gently inched her way forward, finding herself enveloped by warm light, an experience she found surprisingly pleasant and comforting, a sense she not felt since her arrival. The final picture completed. As the aperture contracted behind her, the gallery disintegrated into puzzle sized fragments before the colours ran into a flowing nebulous mist.

A tearful Dane retrieved his fingers from his wife's hand, as he held his son in the other. The monitor had been switched off. Ella had gone.

THE SPLICED CONTINUUM

(Part 1)

She entered the hall to a few glances but no discernible lull in the chatter. There were a couple customary welcome greetings as she perused the books on display. Actually she didn't know anyone there, had simply booked the weekend to get away for a word adventure: a room full of budding individuality.

She stumbled across him in a corner, just like little Jack but surrounded by an assortment of thirteen books. He raised his head to a silky tie-dyed green and orange dashiki, alighted on full lips and curious eyes bordered by the biggest afro in the room: the only afro to be precise. She was the vision of an orange tree in full bloom.

"I came here looking for inspiration," she said. "So what's your genre?"

"Believe it or not, I came for inspiration too," he replied, picking up a copy of 'The Two Gentlemen of Verona'. His dark hair fell across his forehead as he raised his head. He handed her the copy.

"Pleased to meet you," she chuckled slightly. "My name is Verona by the way, Verona Shakespeare. How about that!"

Bells chimed in Julian's ears. Somehow he managed to reply, "I'm Julian, Julian Mann."

The pendulum clock on the wall stopped in mid swing.

(Part 2)

He met her in the room again later and somehow found the courage to ask her if she had any plans for the evening. Between finishing reading, "Black Like Me" and the hotel's cable offering, she replied she was otherwise free. Julian asked what the book was about. She agreed to fill him in over dinner, meeting at 7:30 PM, casual in the lobby where he later found her waiting with one of those large umbrellas. Said she'd borrowed it from the manager of the place on trust. Her hair was back in a bushy ponytail. That simple change made her look so different yet paradoxically just as recognisable. He was captivated by the way her lips parted, sensual, like the way she spoke.

He'd parked the Capri 2.8i with the passenger side nearest the steps so she wouldn't get too wet. They headed for the centre of town.

"Do you drive?"

"I keep meaning to get around to it."

"So you travelled down by train?"

"Uh uh."

They easily found the friendly Chinese restaurant as recommended in the brochure, serving good food with authentic Chinese music playing in the background. They opted for chopsticks, a challenge for Verona. Those serene almond eyes of hers drew him in, put him at ease.

"So what do you do when not trying to write?" She asked him.

"I'm a copywriter for an ad agency."

"Oh right. A lot of fun?"

"As much as I can make it. How about you?"

"I work for a children's charity."

"Must be rewarding."

"It also pays the rent." She nodded warmly.

She explained the book she was reading was about a white man who made himself black to record his experiences. Julian said he'd be interested in reading it. His closest circle of friends did not in fact include anyone of colour. Those people he did come into contact with over time, had only been for casual acquaintance. He found her company disarmingly engaging and challenging. He couldn't explain it, he only knew he did not want to resist. She had a spark that seemed to tap something latent in him. He dropped her off at her hotel.

"I can drive you back to London if you want," he eagerly offered.

"Oh, I already bought a return train ticket, thanks." His heart stopped. "But you can still have my number." She beamed back and his pulse recharged.

(Part 3)

He met with his friends in their regular pub in Sheen later that week: Lionel was a photographer and a mate from their student days. Blake was a former work colleague and Jonathan the pharmaceutical drug pushing salesman of legitimate means.

"So what exactly did you get up to last weekend Julian? Missed a good party man. Enough blow to take you to Mars and back. And by the way, Emily was there. She asked for you," Blake teased.

"Well, I drove down to Devon for a writers' weekend. Was fun, really enjoyed it."

"What you mean is, you met someone. Go on tell us!"

"For a moment there I almost forgot how transparent I am to you guys."

"So, why are you holding out on us with this mystery woman?" Jonathan asked.

"She … she reminds me of rum and raisin ice cream."

"Rum and what? Wait a minute, don't tell me, don't tell me she's a black chick?" Blake quizzed. Julian took a sip of his drink without answering.

"A what?! He's got to be kidding right?" Lionel was visibly shocked.

"For fuck sake Julian, you can't do that to us! Ah no …"

"No, he doesn't mean to fuck you Lionel, but I think he means to shag her."

"Yeh well his dick might drop off," Blake sniggered.

"Well, it didn't when them slave masters were giving them the nutmeg did it?" Julian banged his empty glass on the counter. He'd done some research on racism, realising how normally it was practised. Reading "Black Like Me" had opened his eyes.

They piped down a notch before Blake asked what Julian meant by his last comment.

Jonathan, who was a drop out med student after all, replied that she probably had a little bit of them in her already, under the skin. After another moment's pause, Blake asked if this black blight on their lives had a name.

"Verona. Her name is Verona. If we get on, you might even get to meet her one day."

"Verona? Sounds positively medieval. Probably lives in Brixton. Can you really see yourself ducking and diving just not to get mugged mate? Going down there to see her I mean," Blake carried on.

"She lives in Battersea mate."

"What, so they don't have muggers there these days?"

"Shut up Blake, for pete's sake. We're nearing the end of the twentieth century. The top muggers wear suits, always have." Jonathan then turned back to Julian. "Might have guessed it was something Shakespearean turned your lights on Julian," he remarked. "Takes us back to our student theatre days at uni. You blacked up as Othello, as there wasn't anyone suitable in the group to play the part." He pointed at Julian's chest.

"Yeh, I remember it well," casting back.

Blake wasn't finished with bringing Emily back to Julian's thoughts.

"So, what did happen between you and Emily thingamy anyway?"

"She talked too much about nothing and everything all at once, rather like you Blake. Why don't you try her for size?"

"I don't need you to tell me who to pull Julian!" As soon as the words escaped his mouth, Blake realised he'd backed himself into his own corner.

"Look guys, I'd love to keep sparing with you, but I have a date. Will have to catch you later." With that, Julian exited the bar.

"Oooh," they cooed in chorus after him, wanting him to stay to share more lascivious cocoa details.

They were an unwitting and respectable riot. Alcohol's ability to loosen tongues and unchain social restraints was after all commonplace among friends who thrived under the glass dome of class ridden white alpha male supremacy, successfully so for generations. The Race Relations Act and Scarman's report was not going to miraculously change acquired behaviours with a few sound bites and a clean up of Brixton. Julian knew this unequivocally. He was taking his own steps to brake with this tacit code tugging at his heart.

Julian and Verona dated and dated. When they first went clubbing, she laughed at the way he jerked his body around and had had to teach him how to move more with the rhythms and riddim. He gradually caught the hang of it.

In return, he said he would teach her to ride a bicycle, not drive – she'd have to sort that one herself. He was beginning to think she had a complex about being in control of anything with wheels. She accepted his offer this time.

He cycled from Richmond to Clapham Common on his trusted mountain bike, using the back roads to avoid traffic. It was exhilarating. He didn't ride as often as he wanted. Verona had provided an excuse to improve on that. He spotted her approaching the rendezvous point just as she was preparing to put her walkman back on. He called out to her, his voice full, energised, bounced through the moist air. She turned to see him, waved smiling. He smiled and waved back, completing the connection as he levelled the grass between them. She was wearing a black beret, a warm woolly jacket over a snug pair of black knee length pants, sky blue leg warmers covered her knees ending in trainers.

"Good timing," he breathed. It was 10:30 AM, the Saturday grass was dewy. Nearby a group of youngsters were chasing down a football.

"A bit nippy this morning" she remarked as he dismounted. "You warm enough in that gear of yours?" The ride had heated his sleekly clad, slightly ectomorphic body.

"Yeah. Once you get going, you'll warm up too." He drew in some air and breathed out before he lent over and gave her a light kiss on the cheek. Despite her complaint, her skin felt warm, smooth and yielding to his fleeting touch. He felt quite pumped.

"What were you listening to?" He nodded at her walkman. He was at least four inches taller than her, steady, his black and green gear framed a proud hint of muscles while displaying a defined rear.

"Oh, It's Squeeze. Black Coffee in Bed."

He laughed. "Can't say I've had that pleasure."

Verona bit her lips. "Hmm, let's see how good you are at teaching me to ride aye?" He was already adjusting the saddle slightly downwards to match her height. He handed her his helmet and retrieved a pair of knee and elbow pads from the bag he'd carried on his back.

"All of this?"

"I don't want to have to wheel you home."

"Have a little faith Julian," she pleaded.

He had been surprised when she had told him she'd also never ridden a bike. When she was done kitting up, he ran through the rudiments of steering and braking, then helped her to mount, one hand innocently slipping onto her firm thigh, the other steadied the handle bar as she started to wobble.

"Relax. I've got you. Just try to balance and when you're ready, start pedalling. You'll get the hang of it." He spoke in that adventurous, consoling comprehensive schooled voice of his. Despite this, her dignity slipped several times, fortunately not to ground.

Gradually her confidence grew and half an hour in, Julian let go of the bars and listened to her screams as she gravitated towards the nearest tree that just wouldn't move out of the way. He caught her before she hit it. She flung grateful arms around his neck. They hugged as if glued for it seemed a mini eternity. It had been unintentional, but this was not the time for anything more. He checked if she was ready to get back on the saddle. She giggled to hide her embarrassment, but nodded her nervous determination, their attraction fully established. He simply rubbed her back.

She'd only had a glass of orange before heading out that morning, so they decided to park his bike at hers before heading off for a greasy spoon lunch, weaving through the busy market crowd on the Northcote Road. They ordered scrambled eggs, mushrooms, beans and tomatoes twice, none too greasy after all. Though neither was vegetarian, the protein was agreeably sufficient.

They caught up with what they'd shared over the weeks. He'd finished reading Howard Griffin's "Black Like Me" and had found it moving. He confessed it had given him a sharper perspective on everyday realities of racial issues. At school, his closest friends had been exclusively white, at uni too. Black and Asians students had been passing acquaintances only. They featured more when playing football, cricket and when discussions on Apartheid came up; otherwise a normally contained subject.

"I might not live in the Deep South of America or in South Africa. My family come from Jamaica so the history is comparable. Depending on where this, whatever this is that's happening between us Julian, I don't want you to have any illusions about the reality. This society we live in, historically is neither equal nor fair with its blueprint imprinted world over."

Their beverages arrived, his black coffee without the bed and a small pot of Jasmine tea for Verona. He reached for the white sugar. She suggested he try the Demerara instead. It was the colour of her skin. He found the taste less sweet but the flavour, richer. She poured Demerara in her tea as well.

"Verona, I pretty much think I know what I'm getting into here. I realise you don't want to feel as if my interest in you is just sampling?" He licked his spoon, searched her passionate eyes. "You're a real honest to goodness person to me. I'm investing real time here. But I have feelings too. I just hope you'll give me the chance to show you that." He fed her a piece of hot buttered brown toast. She bit it, slowly.

"Besides, you're too fit to miss. Must be all that salsa dancing you do." If she was a car, in ad terms, he'd compare her to a Jag.

"You must come to one of the classes Julian. I guarantee you'll love it, but you'd have to start with the novices."

"So do you have a steady partner?" What he really wanted to know was would he come up against any competition for her affection.

"It varies week to week. I could make an exception in your case though."

"Oh.?"

Neither had ever gravitated this close to someone of another categorised race. They revelled in watching each other goof up: mapped the other's expressions and bodylines; a chemistry seeping out of their pores: mixing, a new composition playing out.

"I like your ears Julian. They're a lot like mine, but lighter of course. Close to your head, not big and your ridges are inside. I'm hoping it's a sign you're good at listening too. Oh, I also like the fact you don't have a flat bum." She complimented.

"I just think you're beautiful and I don't care how corny that may sound."

He wished he had time to explore their respective anatomical features more, but his gap year sister Olivia was returning from Australia and he was meeting her at Heathrow. He did however quickly acquaint himself with her loo, when he picked up his bike, as he was by then bursting. He kissed her Demerara sweet mouth. She cupped his face with her hands and swept his hair back behind his neat ears.

"I'll be sure to have some Jamaican Blue Mountain coffee next time you come."

"I can't wait to try some."

The inevitable happened after they'd been to the theatre one evening to watch 'The Colored Museum' at the Royal Court in Sloane Square. As a series of vignettes, the sets wove satirical and realistic dramatisations of the African American experience over time – the portrayals symbolically bursting black and blue with passion. The set changes were almost seamlessly done, given the circumstantial practicalities. They enjoyed the programme, absorbed the challenges it exposed for their budding relationship.

It was not something they had planned to happen, certainly not after seeing the play. It was crazy; of all the nights … They didn't speak about the play outside of the theatre, having had animated exchanges about it in the intermission. He had driven her back to hers, followed her indoors. There were no words: it just happened. They made love for the first time, bodies moulding, breaking through a time honoured barrier at a penetrative cellular level with the mutual freedom to just let go.

(Part 4)

Breaking the news of their relationship to their respective parents months later, would prove a bigger test than breaking it to friends however. A course of "Guess Who's Coming for Dinner" and all the rest did not aid matters. His parents had never holidayed in the Caribbean, never tasted salt fish and what's it – ackee. It looked like baby's puke to them. And of course, could they even have children together anyway? Being Jamaicans, such remarks really angered her mother. All that sugar and spice everyone now took for granted, weighing in historically from such roots of human depravity, the truth be known. Fortunately, Olivia was on hand to referee. Not that Julian needed help, before Agnes, having raised her glasses, gave his parents a hiding with the history of slavery and its foster child colonialism. Race, class and the generation gap all featured in the ensuing scrum.

    Her parents' Jamaican accented beef was also to the point: "What? He's not religious? Have you lost your mind? How can he be saved when he doesn't believe in anything? Our daughter to get married in a register office?! Never!"

    After a year's dating and a year's engagement, the Registrar officiated at the compromise reception hall and the Pastor gave the couple a blessing – yes both of them. Rose, Julian's mother, labelled the entire affair a multicultural truce. Now all they had to worry about was how their children would turn out. Was there any chance they could produce one black child and one white to comfort both sides of grandparents? That possibility, though slim – was not impossible.

They honeymooned in Cuba, where they seemed to step back in time. The infrastructure of the country needed rescuing, the cars were a colourful legacy but the people were congenial and the salsa classes paid off for Julian.

Three years down the line and still in keeping with their Shakespearean theme, their first child Miranda was born and two years after that Aaron. Much to everyone's surprise, both children looked Italian. Miranda had curly dark hair while Aaron's was straight. However, both had brown eyes like their parents. Closer inspection proved the children did indeed belong to their parents, as each set of grandparents pointed to distinct family traits.

Miranda was around seven when after returning from school one day, she asked her mother what colour she was.

"What'd you tell her?" Julian asked.

"Why I told her she was the colour of love. Love has no colour and can be any colour you like."

"Why I love you so much Mrs Mann." He tickled his wife. She was extremely ticklish.

All couples have their ups and downs with time. Things began to unravel after Julian started an entirely new job. He began working late, drinking more and became more secretive. Then one day they went out to a posh restaurant with the children. They had not too long arrived, had read the menu when Julian suddenly announced they had to leave.

"Julian what d'you mean we have to go? I'm hungry, the children are too."

"There's somewhere better not too far from here. Come on guys, let's move now!"

Verona, didn't want to cause a scene in front of the children. Some people were being seated to the back of the restaurant and she sensed it had something to do with their entrance. Later when she pressed him about the incident he just apologised and clammed up.

A rift was widening between them. Then the phone calls started, someone would call and then hang up. Sometimes the person – male – called to speak to Secret Squirrel and other times asked for Captain Scarlet. Julian thought the person probably just kept dialling a wrong number and decided to say something funny rather than simply hanging up. Verona was not convinced however, finding the whole business scary especially at night when he sometimes worked late. Julian had their number changed but the calls continued. By this time Verona had had enough. She also complained she felt she was being followed in the supermarket by a man in a Burberry. She had noticed his suspicious behaviour several times. The last time he followed her down the feminine hygiene aisle and was still following when she walked to the baby food section. She was scared for the children. Her husband's offhand response was that she was always ultra sensitive around a particular time of month which did not go down well with his wife. He further deduced that perhaps she was feeling broody again and this was her mind's unconscious way of alerting her to the fact. Verona had responded by first screaming and then breaking the egg she was about to scramble on her forehead; a measure of how ridiculous he was making her feel on top of everything else. He attempted to help clean her face as he would one of the children's but she brushed him off, ordering him to leave her presence while she tried best not to succumb to an impending nervous breakdown.

She was convinced his job was affecting their lives in a negative way. As she no longer felt safe with him around on that account, for the sake of the children, she suggested he move out altogether, to see if that would also improve their fractured communication problems. Though reluctant to do this, Julian agreed to a trial separation. They didn't know quite how to explain the situation to the in-laws. Everyone was flummoxed. The children were extremely upset. They just didn't understand what was happening.

The couple later came to the arrangement that Julian would have the children at weekends as often as he could. Verona laid her cards out, she wanted him to give up his private investigation work so he could come home. As the weeks passed, it finally occurred to him that he had possibly become addicted to the intrigue, danger and money he was making. Though his fifteen year marriage was on the rocks, he found he just could not stop himself.

Lionel had introduced him to this line after the Ad agency Julian worked for merged with a larger outfit and he was typically selected as part of the fat they had to cut for younger, leaner boys and girls for less pay. He had taken the redundancy money, opting to work freelance for these clandestine ex-forces, ex-CID types who were in the mushrooming PI game which Julian joined as a stop-gap. It was hard to tell if any of them knew anymore where the lines between good and bad were, whether these had ever existed for them. He wouldn't count any of his new acquaintances as friends. Harper, his main contact, was a relic and more moustache than man. He spoke to Julian in a condescending way Julian tried best not to respond to. He rattled off their dodgy meetings with: "Am I making myself clear enough Mr Mann? We don't want any traces left for anyone to draw attention, that there's been any scouting around if you follow." The pompous port-bellied arsehole, Julian hoped he suffered from gout. All he was required to do was some discreet background checks, photographs, nothing fancy or risky like burglary for goodness sake. Just a bit of paid prying, what it all boiled down to, plus it paid the mortgage.

One evening when he called his wife, she told him she'd bumped into his friend Blake outside their house. Blake was recently divorced and was apparently just driving past. Julian did not need to hear this.

"You sure about that? Just bumping into him I mean."

"You trying to suggest something Julian? Who that dumb ass?"

"I hope you didn't invite him into our house while I wasn't there. Blake is a cockroach." Some dumb asses specialised in talking the pants off women. This Julian knew. Blake having met Verona on various occasions over the years, Julian had not been blind to the way Blake sometimes looked at her on the sly. He wasn't past taking a crack at a woman when she was vulnerable and to finally stick it to him too.

"No I did not invite him in" she stressed. And before you ask, the children were at school Ok?"

"I don't want any of my friends in my house or around my children when I'm not there. You don't know them like I do. Understand?" Engaging a child would be plan B to indirectly hook said female and all just to prove he could, race no longer being an issue.

"Loud and clear Julian."

They still slept together when the children were with the grandparents. She wasn't seeing anyone during their separation – he would have known and would probably strangle anyone who came around his kids. Besides, when she was in the mood, she hightailed it round to his. A hard habit to break, especially in springtime and he was only too willing to oblige when he could juggle his schedule. It was stupid.

"I didn't marry a secret agent. I married a copywriter who had dreams of becoming an author."

"Pardon me, but seems you like sleeping with 007 types."

"You telling me you work for M15 now? You admitting that Julian?"

"I'm kidding, just kidding. I'm not admitting to anything."

"That's the problem. Get from top of me. I'll wash when I get home. You can collect the children from your parents and bring them back to the house."

"Fine." He rolled over again. No second helping today.

She opened the door on her way out, slamming it after Einstein his new cat shot up the stairs. He watched her drive away in her Peugeot.

A couple weeks later and no sex in between, divorce papers dropped on his mat. The no sex part must have come from her mother, religious fruit bat as she was Julian reflected. This was becoming expensive and serious.

When they spoke on the phone Verona admitted filing divorce papers to ram home his reality check. Anything could happen and none of it had played any part in why they'd got married and had children in the first place. It had been some time after the job with R&P had first come up. Later, after the publicised bloodbath event at their offices on 19th May, Julian found he had finally come full circle. His life was a continuum mess. He needed his family back. They made sense to him. He wanted the lawyers gone for certain - leeches. If ever there was a tribe that danced to the tune of the Master of Deceit it was surely them. To Julian they were marionettes in a tangle of chains, breaking rules everyone else was expected to ignorantly live by; loophole bandits. He could well do without shelling out to one of their overpaid handshakes.

He missed his children fulltime and truth was, wanted his wife back, for better or worse.

Between sleeping and waking, Julian's occupation had oscillated on a string which led him to *'The Tickled*

Bird'. He drew his loose dressing gown tighter as if for more security, Anita Ward singing "Ring My Bell" reverberated in his head for some bizarre reason. He rang his wife back, his voice coarse as gravel, as if he'd been trapped down a mine shaft. She listened quietly as he told her he was coming home.

"Yes, Miranda thought you'd be back soon. I knew it was only a matter of time Julian. Hurry back. I'll fix lunch and tell the children."

ENIGMA

From whence comes pain?

From near and far
Day and night
From places shallow, places deep
It surfaces

Why do you smile?

From remembrance old,
Some recent, vague, new
Things lost, things found
Reconciled in moments

How do you grow?

In abundance to waste
From indifference to care
And challenges grave
Trials we share

Where is love?

Betwixt space in togetherness
There and back
A feeling sustained
Love is a sense

From whence it came